To

Luna,

MERRY CHRISTMAS!

Love from

....

Gingerbread
Town

Luna sees a present
wrapped up neatly with a bow.
The label has a name,
and the wrapping seems to glow.

"This present is for me!" cries Luna,
with the biggest grin.

Luna opens it to look inside,
and suddenly falls in!

Luna's in the frosty woods,
looking at blue skies.
To find a world inside a box
is such a big surprise!

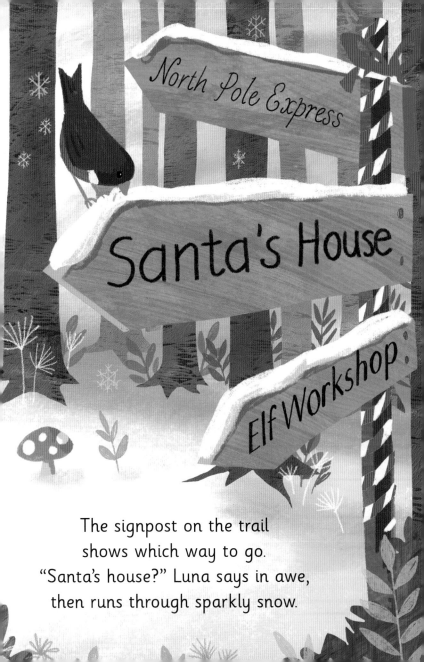

The signpost on the trail
shows which way to go.
"Santa's house?" Luna says in awe,
then runs through sparkly snow.

Luna spots a village
and a family up ahead.
Luna gasps and can't believe,
they're made of gingerbread!

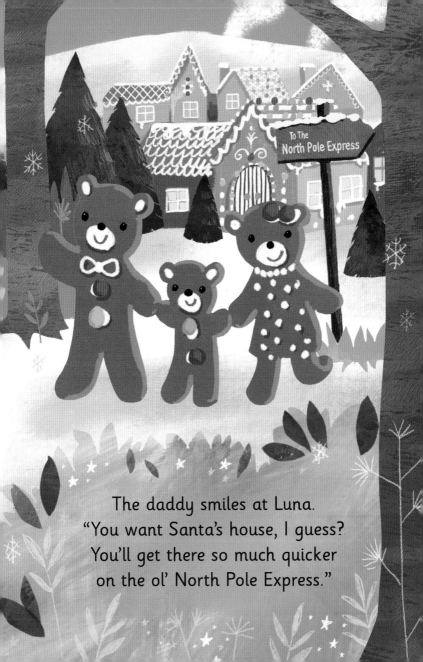

The daddy smiles at Luna.
"You want Santa's house, I guess?
You'll get there so much quicker
on the ol' North Pole Express."

Luna's at the station
and spots a little elf.
The elf exclaims, "I'm off to see
Santa Claus, himself."

Luna is excited.
"Yes, I'm off to see him too!
But I'm not sure which way to go.
Can I come along with you?"

They hear a distant chugging sound,
then see the train appear.
The elf says, "Luna, this is it!
The North Pole Express is here!"

A small penguin conductor
brings the steam train to a stop.
"All aboard!" he shouts to Luna.
"Come ride with me up top."

Luna has the perfect seat
and an even better view.
Snowy forests whiz on by,
while the chimney toots *"choo-choo!"*

They reach their destination.
Luna's face is full of cheer.
The penguin blows his whistle,
shouting, "Hooray! We are here!"

The elf takes Luna to a house.
Mrs. Claus greets them with glee.
"I'm so glad you are here at last.
Come in and sit with me!"

Santa's House

Luna sips hot chocolate,
and eats warm cookies from a plate.
The elf says, "Luna, we must go.
We really can't be late."

Luna is led through
a busy workshop full of elves,
where a million shiny toys
sit high on countless shelves.

"Will I see Santa?" Luna hopes.
"I think that would be neat."
The elf says, "Yes! That's why you're here.
He really wants to meet!"

"Yes, you wished to meet me.
I made that wish come true.
And now, I have a special toy.
One I made...just for you."

Luna peeks inside the box.
What could this present be?
Santa magically disappears,
and Luna's by the tree.

The trip has been amazing,
a night Luna won't forget.
And in the box is Santa's gift:
a North Pole Express train set!

Luna, hop on board the
NORTH POLE EXPRESS!

Draw yourself and your friends
on the train to see Santa.

Written by J.D. Green
Illustrated by Joanne Partis
Designed by Ryan Dunn

Copyright © Bidu Bidu Books Ltd. 2022

Put Me In The Story is a
registered trademark of Sourcebooks, Inc.
All rights reserved.

Published by Put Me In The Story,
a publication of Sourcebooks.
P.O. Box 4410, Naperville, Illinois 60567-4410
(630) 536-1104
www.putmeinthestory.com

Date of Production: June 2022
Run Number: 5025359
Printed and bound in Italy (LG)
10 9 8 7 6 5 4 3 2 1

MIX
Paper from
responsible sources
FSC® C023419
FSC
www.fsc.org

put me
in the story

Bestselling books starring your child!

www.putmeinthestory.com